ZARA'S
RULES
for
Finding
HIDDEN
TREASURE

ZARA'S RULES for Finding

HIDDEN TREASURE

HENA KHAN

Illustrated by Wastana Haikal

SALAAM READS

NEW YORK | LONDON | TORONTO
SYDNEY | NEW DELHI

SALAAM
READS

An imprint of Simon & Schuster Children's Publishing Division
1230 Avenue of the Americas, New York, New York 10020
This book is a work of fiction. Any references to historical events,
real people, or real places are used fictitiously. Other names, characters, places,
and events are products of the author's imagination, and any resemblance to actual
events or places or persons, living or dead, is entirely coincidental.
Text © 2022 by Hena Khan
Jacket and interior illustrations © 2022 by Wastana Haikal
Jacket design by Laura Eckes © 2022 by Simon & Schuster, Inc.
All rights reserved, including the right of reproduction in whole or in part in any form.
SALAAM READS and its logo are trademarks of Simon & Schuster, Inc.
For information about special discounts for bulk purchases, please contact Simon & Schuster
Special Sales at 1-866-506-1949 or business@simonandschuster.com.
The Simon & Schuster Speakers Bureau can bring authors to your live event.
For more information or to book an event, contact the Simon & Schuster Speakers Bureau
at 1-866-248-3049 or visit our website at www.simonspeakers.com.
Also available in a Salaam Reads paperback edition.
Interior design by Tom Daly
The text for this book was set in Adobe Caslon Pro.
The illustrations for this book were rendered digitally.
Manufactured in the United States of America
0922 FFG
First Salaam Reads hardcover edition October 2022
2 4 6 8 10 9 7 5 3 1
Library of Congress Cataloging-in-Publication Data
Names: Khan, Hena, author. | Haikal, Wastana, illustrator.
Title: Zara's rules for finding hidden treasure / Hena Khan ; illustrated by Wastana Haikal.
Description: First Salaam Reads hardcover edition. | New York : Salaam Reads, 2022. |
Audience: Ages 7-10 | Audience: Grades 4-6 | Summary: After Zara's bike goes missing, her parents
insist on her earning money to pay for it, so she and her friend Naomi turn their red wagon into
The Treasure Wagon and try and sell some old knickknacks found in her family's basement.
Identifiers: LCCN 2021047125 | ISBN 9781534497627 (hardcover) | ISBN 9781534497610
(paperback) | ISBN 9781534497634 (ebook)
Subjects: CYAC: Pakistani Americans—Fiction. | Muslims—United States—Fiction. | Business
enterprises—Fiction. | Friendship—Fiction.
Classification: LCC PZ7.K526495 Zak 2022 | DDC [Fic]—dc23
LC record available at https://lccn.loc.gov/2021047125

To all my friends who made ours a wonderful

neighborhood to grow up in together

ZARA'S RULES for Finding HIDDEN TREASURE

CHAPTER 1

* * *

"Hurry up!" Jade yells.

My legs burn as I keep pedaling. I'm only halfway up the biggest hill on the way to Radley's Park. And I'm slowing down no matter how hard I try to go faster.

"Come *on!*" Jade is waiting for me at the top of the hill. The sparkly pink tassels on her bike handles flutter in the cool fall breeze. She crosses her arms impatiently.

I reach for the water bottle clipped onto the side of my bike and take a sip. My old bike didn't have a clip. It also squeaked and rattled, and the chain kept falling off. Plus it was getting so small for me that my knees hit the handlebars. Luckily, Mama and Baba surprised me with this new bike, in a perfect shade of blue, right before school started. But this hill is still as hard as ever.

"Al . . . most . . . there . . . ," Naomi pants behind me. I focus on the back of Gloria's helmet in front of us as she reaches her older sister first.

And then a few moments later, we make it! I mop the sweat off my face and gaze at the path winding through the park.

"Finally!" Jade smiles. "Let's go." It's obvious that my neighbor loves being the one in charge on our long bike rides. We're only allowed to come this far without a grown-up because Jade's thirteen and old enough to babysit. Not that we're babies *or* need sitting.

Naomi and I are both ten, and Gloria's almost twelve. But Jade took an official babysitting class and earned a certificate for doing CPR recently. That means she knows how to help people if they stop breathing. A moment ago, when I was gasping for air, I thought I might actually need

Jade's services. But now I've caught my breath, and I'm ready to play.

Ever since they redid the equipment at Radley's, it's the best park in the area. There's a huge pirate ship with big twisty slides, a fake plank, and tire swings. Because of the foamy soft padding on the ground, you don't get hurt if you fall down. The only bad part about Radley's being so awesome is that it's popular . . . a little *too* popular. People swarm to it on the weekends. And that means we have to wait for the swings and dodge all the little kids learning how to scooter and Rollerblade on the foam.

"What do you want to do first?" Naomi asks as we park our bikes in the crowded rack. I carefully slide mine into the slot next to hers, making sure it doesn't get scratched. When my friend takes off her helmet, her usually puffy curls are flattened to the sides of her head.

"Pirate ship hide-and-seek!" Gloria suggests.

"Snack time!" Jade points to her backpack, which is decorated with patches from national parks. "I've got clementines and pretzels."

"How about hide-and-seek and then snacks?" I offer. "I'll be it."

"Okay! Zara's it!" Naomi says.

I close my eyes and count to twenty while the girls scatter. When I open my eyes again, the girls are all hidden. Last time we played, we decided the trash can area is off-limits, so I don't check there. But the bushes next to them have a little gap between them.

Sure enough, I spot silver glinting off a sneaker between the leaves. Naomi's in there, curled up into a tiny ball.

"I see you, Naomi!" I yell.

"You always find me first!" Naomi complains. It's true. Naomi is full of great ideas, except when it comes to thinking of hard-to-find hiding places. And half the time her colorful clothes make it easier to track her down.

"Two more." I scan the playground. There's a spot in the pirate ship that's shaped like a tube.

"Look." I point. "I bet one of them is hiding in there."

As I'm running toward the ship, I hear my name.

"Hey, Zara!"

I whip my head around. It's Alan, my next-door neighbor, wearing a bright green soccer uniform.

"Oh, hi, Alan. Do you have practice?"

"A game. We lost. What are you doing?"

"Hide-and-seek with the girls. Want to play?"

"Sure."

"Alan!" Mrs. Goodman calls from the field. "We need to go!" She's holding a bag, a cooler, and a folding chair.

"Can I play a little?"

"For a few minutes. We're going to Aunt Christina's, remember? Hi, Zara! How are you, sweetie?"

Before I can answer, we're interrupted by the shrill music of the ice cream truck. As it pulls into the parking lot, kids scream and race toward it like it's giving away free puppies. Even Jade and Gloria pop out from their hiding places and run to get into line. Jade always stashes a little money in her backpack in case of an emergency—and the ice cream truck is definitely an emergency.

"Can I get ice cream?" Alan asks his mom.

"If the line moves quickly." Mrs. Goodman reaches

into her purse and hands Alan a few dollars. "Zara, you get something too."

"Thank you, Mrs. G.!" All the parents on our street look out for each other's kids. Mama says it's what makes our neighborhood the best to grow up in, and I agree.

I study the menu on the side of the truck.

"One cookies-and-cream bar, please," I tell the man, who hands it to me with a wink and gives Alan his change.

"I have to go," Alan says as he tears open the wrapper of his ice cream sandwich. "See you later."

"Thanks for the ice cream." I wave and then walk to a bench with the girls to eat our treats.

"What do you want to do now?" Jade asks after we've finished. Her mouth and tongue are completely blue from her raspberry Popsicle. "The slide?"

"Yeah!" We all jump up, energized by the sugar, and spend the next couple of hours sliding, swinging, and playing tag. It's basically a perfect afternoon.

"Oh no! It's almost four," Jade says, checking her phone. "I promised we'd be home by then. We have to go . . . now!"

Luckily, the ride home is almost all downhill, so it should be faster than getting here. We head over to the bike rack, making plans for when we'll return to the park.

"Wait a second." Naomi grabs my arm. "Where's your bike? Didn't you put it with mine?"

"What?" My heart thumps wildly as I scan the rack. I'm certain I put it right next to her bike. But now it's not there.

"Maybe someone moved it?" Gloria suggests. But I run up and down the rack and search the grass around us, and don't see it anywhere. It feels like there's a gigantic Popsicle stick stuck in my throat.

My beautiful, brand-new bike is . . . gone.

CHAPTER 2

* * *

"How could this happen?" Jade asks. "Didn't you lock it?"

"No," I mutter as angry, hot tears roll down my face.

Gloria turns around to face me, a hand resting on her hip. "Wait. What? You didn't lock your brand-new bike?" she asks. "Why not?"

"I never locked my old one." My voice is shaky, and I sit on the curb by the bike rack.

"Yeah, but no one would want to take that one. It was beat-up, and made so much noise that we could hear you coming from a mile away," Gloria says. "I mean, no offense."

"I know. I think my dad took it to the dump. He didn't think anyone would want it either," I tell her.

Naomi still hasn't stopped searching the rack. For the third time she carefully examines the handful of bikes left, as if one of them is magically going to turn into mine.

"I can't believe it!" I wail. "What kind of person would take a bike that doesn't belong to them? My water bottle even has my name on it!"

"Should we call the police?" Jade asks. "Or your parents?"

"What can they do?" Naomi asks.

"I don't know." Jade shrugs. "Help us find whoever took it?"

"Maybe someone took it by mistake," Naomi says, sitting next to me on the curb. The thought stirs a flicker of hope inside me.

"Maybe!" I stand up. "That *must* be it!"

"I mean, yeah, I guess that could maybe be what happened," Gloria says, although the way she squishes up half her face makes it seem like she doesn't quite believe it.

"Listen, Gloria and I have to get home," Jade says, tapping into her phone super quickly, the way teenagers do. "What do you want to do, Zara? Do you want to call your parents to come pick you up? Or walk home?"

Now that she's got that babysitting certificate, Jade actually *does* seem more responsible than usual.

"I'll walk," I decide. I'm not ready to tell my parents what happened yet.

"I'll walk with you," Naomi quickly volunteers.

"Are you sure?" Gloria asks. She looks back and forth at her older sister and us.

"Yeah," I say.

"Are you going to be okay?" Jade confirms.

"Yeah," I repeat, and take a deep breath. "I'll be fine."

"Okay, we'll see you later," Jade says. She gets onto her bike and adjusts her backpack.

"Bye." Gloria straps on her helmet. "Sorry about your bike."

"Don't be sorry yet," Naomi says. "We still might find it."

"Good luck," Gloria says as she pedals off, turning and making one last, sad face.

After they leave, Naomi and I search the entire playground for the bike. We look in the bushes, in the pirate ship, behind the trash cans. It's like a long game of hide-and-seek with no finding. And no fun.

"Let's go home," I finally say. "It's not here."

"Maybe someone'll bring it back tomorrow when they realize they took the wrong bike," Naomi says.

"I hope so. Are you sure you're okay walking?" I ask Naomi.

"Totally," Naomi says. She wheels her bike between us as we start heading home. "What are you going to tell your parents?"

"The truth, I guess." Imagining their reaction makes me sweat. I think about all the times Baba and Mama have told me to be careful with my things. They just got angry with my little brother last weekend for losing his soccer ball after leaving it in the front yard during a storm. Zayd hardly ever gets in trouble for anything.

And he lost an old ball, not a fancy new bike.

"I hope they don't get too mad," Naomi says.

"Me too."

We walk along in silence, lost in our thoughts. I glance at Naomi, grateful for her company. In just the few months since she moved into our neighborhood this summer, she's already become my best friend. And someone that I can't imagine not having around, especially in moments like this.

"Zara!"

As soon as we turn onto our street, my mom calls out to me. She's standing by the mailbox. I didn't even get a chance to figure out what to say to her yet!

"Zara!" she repeats. "Are you hurt? Why are you walking?"

"I'm . . . fine. . . . I . . . um . . ."

"Where's your bike?" Mama's voice is filled with worry as she stares at me.

Naomi quietly turns into her driveway. And I swallow hard as I think about what to say to my mother.

CHAPTER 3

* * *

"What do you mean 'gone'?" Mama shakes her head like she doesn't understand me.

"I mean it was in the bike rack, and then it was . . . gone. Like I said."

"I still don't understand," Mama says. She points to a chair in the kitchen, and I sit down. It's suddenly like I'm in one of those true-crime shows she likes to watch. The light dangling over the table is blinding, and I squint.

"How could it disappear?" Mama adds. "You locked it, right?"

I stare at my fingernail and don't answer her.

"Zara! Are you telling me you didn't lock your bike?"

I shake my head as Zayd runs into the kitchen clutching a toy car.

"You lost your new bike?" he yelps, his eyes extra wide. "Are you in so much trouble?"

"Go away, Zayd!" I snap. "It's none of your business."

"Zara," Mama says with a frown. "Don't speak to your brother that way. Now, this is serious. Tell me exactly what happened."

Baba comes into the room next. Mama tells him what's going on, in a super-annoyed voice.

"Are you kidding me?" My father turns to me. "You seriously didn't lock your bike? Why in the world did we get you a lock, then?"

"I forgot," I mumble. "I never locked my old bike, so I wasn't used to it."

Baba slaps himself on the forehead like he does when he's amazed by how terrible something is. And right now that something is me.

"Unbelievable, Zara! I thought we taught you to take care of your things. And you know the bike was expensive."

"I know." I hang my head and chew on the fingernail now. The tears are back and fill my eyes again.

"Don't bite your nails," Mama scolds as she reaches for the phone. "We should file a police report. What kind of person steals a little kid's bike? In the middle of the afternoon? In a crowded place?"

"That's what I said!" I tell her. Maybe we can focus on how evil this *other* person is instead of on my mistake.

"Well, you certainly made it easy for them by being careless," Baba grumbles.

So much for that.

Mama talks on the phone in the other room for a bit with someone at the police station while Baba lectures Zayd and me about "the value of a dollar," about how "money doesn't grow on trees," and about how "lucky you are" to have nice things. After a few minutes Zayd looks like he's about to cry too, even though he didn't do anything wrong. But that's what he gets for rushing to gloat over my bad luck.

"Okay, well, we'll see what they say," Mama says as she comes back into the kitchen. "But the officer didn't sound very hopeful that we'll find it."

"Do you think someone took it by mistake?" I ask, remembering Naomi's words. "Maybe they thought it was their bike, and it's an honest mix-up."

"Maybe." Mama shrugs.

"Doubtful." Baba's lips are a thin line.

"Should we make signs and put them up in the neighborhood and in the park, just in case?" I suggest.

"We can have a reward!" Zayd adds. "Everyone likes rewards!"

"Good idea, Zayd," I say, feeling bad for growling at him earlier. I imagine someone showing up to collect their reward and delivering the bike to me, as good as new. The thought fills me with relief.

"I guess it doesn't hurt to try," Mama says.

"But if it doesn't work, we aren't getting you another bike," Baba warns. "You'll have to save up for one yourself."

"Like with an allowance?" I've been hoping to start

getting an allowance like some of my friends at school do.

"Good one!" Baba snorts. "If I gave you an allowance, I would still be paying for it. You'll have to *earn* it."

Earn it? Doing what?

"How's a kid supposed to earn money?" Zayd's seven, but he still pronounces it "stupposed to."

"I don't know," Baba says. "But like I said, money doesn't grow on trees. And the sooner you two understand that, the better."

Zayd turns to me, his eyes bugging out of his head. I know he wants us to get out of here before we get another lecture.

"Can we go make the signs now?" I ask.

"Yes. Go." Baba puts his hand on Mama's back, and she sucks on her teeth as if to say, *How did we end up with kids like these?*

Zayd and I spend the next hour until dinner making signs. His tongue sticks out a little as he colors in the letters I draw, and he mostly stays within the lines.

"What are you going to do if no one brings the bike

back?" he asks, his forehead wrinkled with worry. "How are you going to make money?"

"I don't know. I can ask Jade about babysitting."

"You're not babysitting me!" Zayd declares. "Only Jamal Mamoo babysits me. And Naano."

I'm not even offended. When our uncle or grandma take care of us, we have the best time ever. Jamal Mamoo gets us pizza and fizzy lemonade, and Naano makes us parathas and mango milkshakes. We watch movies and Pakistani dramas, and play cards and ludo and stay up late. I don't want to be a babysitter if it means they'll stop coming over. And besides, Baba made it clear he isn't interested in paying me anyway.

"I mean *other* kids, Zayd," I say with a sigh. "Or I don't know. I'll do something else. I just have to figure it out. And quick." I don't want to miss out on having fun with my friends, all of our bike rides, and going to Radley's.

For now I'm still hoping the bike will come home.

CHAPTER 4

* * *

"No one called?" Naomi frowns and shakes her head in disappointment. "After three whole days?"

"Nope," I grumble.

Naomi grabs the broom and sweeps dead leaves out of our clubhouse. We've totally transformed the toolshed Mr. Chapman built before he moved to Florida and Naomi's family moved into his house, across the street from mine. The clubhouse has curtains, string lights, and decorations, and it's the headquarters for all our plans.

"I really thought someone would bring it back," Naomi says, pausing to pick up a tiny pine cone. "Especially with the reward."

"Maybe the reward should have been bigger?" I wonder aloud. "But I think my bike is gone for good, and my parents said they won't get me another one. They're teaching me a *lesson*. I have to earn the money myself."

"Whoa. What are you going to do?"

"I don't know." I stare at the wall of the clubhouse, which has a big whiteboard of our latest neighborhood records. As if it's taunting me, the last record is for "longest bike ride," held by Gloria. How am I supposed to break that now, without a bicycle?

"Maybe we could have a lemonade stand," Naomi suggests. "That could be fun."

I describe the last time we had a lemonade stand, before Naomi moved here. Jade made it extra fancy, since she's the best artist out of all of us. She painted a paper tablecloth and drew a beautiful glittery sign. Gloria got mason jars and filled them with paper straws, and added a

basket filled with homemade cookies that came free with the lemonade. Alan tried to direct all the cars stopped on the corner toward us by yelling and pointing them in our direction.

But in the end our only customers were Jamal Mamoo, our parents, and two nice strangers driving by who paid extra for the cookies. Zayd and little Melvin drank and spilled at least seven cups of lemonade each. And Mama calculated that after all the costs, we probably spent about thirty dollars to make $3.75.

"Okay, maybe not that, then," Naomi agrees. "What if you sell something more expensive than lemonade? Or something that costs less?"

"Like what?"

Naomi points to the pile of rocks on the shelf in the corner. That project kept us busy for a few afternoons. We searched for the smoothest rocks we could find, and painted them with designs, inspirational messages, and silly faces. Melvin still brings us rocks that he finds in his yard. He's the youngest of us, and closest to the ground, so it's probably easiest for him to spot them.

"How about we sell our rocks? They didn't cost us much," she says.

I pick up one of the nicer rocks, which is painted with a rainbow peace sign. I can imagine it sitting on someone's desk, or in their garden. And I bet they'd be willing to pay money for it.

"That's a great idea!" I say. Naomi really is full of good

ideas, like new records to break, fun games to play, and even tasty snacks. And she knows how to make money too?

"We could sell more than the rocks," I add. "I made a bunch of those little baskets in my weaving class. We could sell those, too. And some of our paintings and other crafts."

"It'll be a craft store!" Naomi cheers. "Except instead of supplies for making crafts, we're selling crafts that are already finished."

"Exactly! What should we call it?"

"Something really great, maybe with both of our names in it. Zaomi? Naora?" Naomi's eyebrows come together like they do when she's thinking really hard.

"Um. Let's keep working on it," I say.

I remember that Zayd has an old red wagon he doesn't use anymore. We could use that to display our goods. And that would allow us to travel from house to house, selling stuff on wheels like the ice cream truck, instead of being stuck in one spot like the lemonade stand. The more I think about it, the more I think this is going to work!

"How about the Crafty Kids Art Cart?" I say.

"I like it!" Naomi throws up a victorious fist. "Let's do it!"

I pull out my notebook and start a new page with the words "Rules for the Business." That way, just like for the games we play, we can keep it fair and make sure we all agree on everything *before* any fights.

"Number one: we split all the money we make, no matter whose stuff gets sold," I say.

"That's good," Naomi agrees.

"Number two: we have to go together whenever we sell things."

"Definitely." Naomi nods.

"And number three: we can't let everyone drink up all our profits, like the lemonade stand."

"Got it," Naomi says.

I drag the wagon out of my garage, and we dust it and clean off the cobwebs. But when we put the rocks inside, they sit there in a pile, looking more like trash than something for sale.

"We have to make this nicer," I say, and frown.

"We need Jade," Naomi suggests. "I'll get her."

A few minutes later Jade comes outside. "What's up?" she asks.

"This." I point to the wagon.

Jade peers inside. "Your rocks?"

"Yeah. We're selling them. Can you make this look better, since you're good at that stuff?" I update her on the business plan and remind her of the reason why I have to make money in the first place.

"You definitely need a bike. I'll help." Jade walks around the wagon and pushes out her bottom lip as she thinks.

"Get me a blanket, a cake stand, some dried flowers, and a couple of stuffed animals," she finally says. "Cute ones."

Naomi and I run to collect the items, and after Jade arranges them all, I swear our wagon could be in one of those fancy stores. The kind of place with no customers inside that Mama likes to go into, and then complain later about how expensive it is. Except our stuff isn't expensive at all. We decide that everything is for sale for two dollars each, or three items for five dollars.

This is going to be a huge success. I can feel it. I'm going to be back on another new bike in no time.

CHAPTER 5

* * *

Jamal Mamoo sits next to me on the front step, after carefully making sure there's no bird droppings or dirt on it. I know he's going to try to make me laugh. My uncle thinks joking around is how everything gets better. But it's not going to work right now. Because my business is a complete failure. And even worse, my friends went on a bike ride this afternoon without me.

"Come on, Zara." Jamal Mamoo nudges me with his elbow. "Are you trying to tell me that people don't want to pay good money for rocks and straw? I refuse to believe it."

"It's not just rocks and straw, Mamoo! It's art!" I sniff.

"I see that. You've made a very impressive and artful display." Jamal Mamoo points to the wagon and nods his appreciation.

"Jade did that part."

"Well, then Jade's got talent."

I have to agree with him. But that doesn't change the fact that everything went wrong anyway. Naomi and I dragged the wagon up and down the block and rang at least twenty doorbells for the past two days. Only four people opened their doors. Sometimes we heard footsteps inside and knew our neighbors were peeping at us from their windows or through their cameras. And even though we waved and held up our sign, they still ignored us.

"So, you had no takers at all?" Jamal Mamoo asks.

"Well, Mrs. Goodman took a rock with a sunset painted on it. She said she could use it as a doorstop."

That makes Jamal Mamoo chuckle.

"It's not funny!" I protest.

But that makes him laugh harder.

"Your art is on the floor propping open a door," he says. And when he breaks into his famous extra-loud snorty laugh, it's impossible not to laugh along with him. I start to giggle, despite myself.

"The lady with the husky named Tala took a basket," I add.

That makes Jamal Mamoo laugh even harder. "Let's hope it doesn't become a pooper scooper." He whoops.

"MAMOO!" I squeal. "That's so gross! And it's NOT."

I pause.

"I mean, it better not be!" I add.

"Okay, okay, I'm sure it's not. Sorry," he says, wiping his eyes. Jamal Mamoo isn't that much younger than Mama, but she always says her younger brother is basically a big kid in a grown-up body. "I think you might need to change your strategy." Jamal Mamoo puts on a serious face.

"What do you mean?"

"The arts and crafts are cute, but you might want to move into higher value items that people are willing to spend money on."

"But I don't have the money to buy items with a higher value! If I did, I'd buy myself a bike," I argue.

"Good point." Now my uncle gets up and starts to pace.

"Are you hungry?" Mama sticks her head out the front door. "I'm making chai."

"I'll take some chai as long as there are cookies," Jamal Mamoo says.

"I wish I could just sell stuff that no one wants," I mutter.

"People do it all the time." Jamal Mamoo chuckles. "Ever hear of a garage sale? Like they say, one person's trash is another person's treasure."

"That's it!" I slap my leg. "I'll have a garage sale. Except I'll use the wagon instead of the garage."

"That's genius," Jamal Mamoo says. "People make lots of money reselling goods. Some make entire businesses out of it." Now he's getting excited.

We head inside for chai and cookies. I drink milk instead of chai, since tea has caffeine in it, and I'm not allowed. And because it tastes gross.

"Mama," I begin while Jamal Mamoo sips his tea. "Do you have things you don't need that I could sell, like for a garage sale? The arts-and-crafts sale only got us four dollars. Oh, wait. Actually, five dollars."

"Did you have another customer you forgot about?" Jamal Mamoo asks as he shoves an entire cookie into his mouth and chews.

"No. This man on the end of the street gave us a dollar because he was nice. Or maybe he was confused about what we were doing. I wasn't sure."

Mama and Jamal Mamoo look at each other and smile.

"I think I can find some things for you," Mama says. "But are you sure you want to host a garage sale? Trust me, it's a lot of work."

"I thought I could keep using the wagon. Then we don't have to wait for people to come to our driveway."

"Hmmm." Mama ponders the idea, but I can tell she likes it.

"You'd better make sure the neighbors don't get upset with you for ringing their doorbells," Jamal Mamoo warns.

"Maybe you can walk up and down and ring a bell or play music to get their attention instead."

"Like the ice cream man!" I say. "That's what I was thinking too!"

"Exactly." Jamal Mamoo high-fives me. "And now I'm in the mood for ice cream to go with this cookie. Got any?"

I get him the tub of mint chocolate chip, while Mama complains he's going to spoil his appetite for dinner. She tells me where to find items to sell, in some boxes in the basement. And then I head over to Naomi's house right as she's returning from her bike ride with Gloria and Jade. Her face is a little guilty as she parks her bike. But when I fill her in on the new plan, she gets excited. And Mrs. Goldstein is happy to share even more things for us to sell.

"This is fantastic, girls!" she cheers. "I meant to find a home for these before we moved, but never did, and they ended up with us here."

I check over the box of candlesticks, antique perfume bottle, photo album, dusty globe-shaped bookends, and uneven handmade bowls. Someone is going to want this stuff. Even if it's to prop up a plant or feed their dogs. Like Jamal Mamoo said, one person's trash is another's treasure. Or, sometimes, maybe the other way around.

CHAPTER 6

***

As I try to arrange the items on the wagon in the garage as nicely as Jade did, Naano and Nana Abu come shuffling up the driveway. Nana Abu is carrying a glass bowl covered with foil.

"Let me take that, Nana Abu," I say, and grab the dish from my grandfather. It's surprisingly heavy.

"Thank you, beti," he says, and pats me on the head.

"What is it?" I ask.

"I made gulab jamun," Naano says. "Your favorite."

"Yum! Thanks!" Naano is always bringing us treats,

and Mama complains that they have too much sugar
or salt or fat. Then Naano grumbles that you need all
those things for food to have any taste. Usually, as they
argue, Nana Abu quietly eats a whole bunch of whatever the food is. And then they both unite to scold him,
while he sits back and pats his belly and smiles. He and
I both love gulab jamun the most, and I can't wait to
eat them.

"What's cooking?" Nana Abu asks as he walks into
the house and sniffs the air.

"I made Thai curry," Mama says. She uncovers the
pot, and Nana Abu peers inside.

"Smells good," he says.

"Asalaamualaikum!" Zayd yells as he runs into the
kitchen and barrels into our grandparents with hugs.
"Are you here because of the bike?"

"What bike?" Naano says.

"Zara lost her bike," Zayd explains as I shove him.
"Ow! No pushing!"

"You lost your bike?" Nana Abu turns to me. "How?"

"The new one?" Naano says. "When?"

"You don't have to tell everyone, Zayd," I grumble.

"We aren't *everyone*," Naano says, shushing me. "Tell us what happened."

"Everything is fine, Ami," Mama says. She hands Zayd a handful of forks and napkins and glares at him. "Set the table, please, and learn to let Zara share her own news."

"Yeah, Zayd," I agree, glad that Mama is taking my side today.

We sit down to eat, and I haven't put a scoop of rice on my plate yet when Naano brings it up again.

"What about your bike?"

"Let the child eat," Nana Abu says.

"She can eat and talk," Naano insists.

"My bike was stolen when I went to the park, Naano. I didn't lock it. But I'm going to be more responsible in the future. And I'm going to earn enough money to buy another bike." I tell her the whole story in one breath because I don't really want to talk about it again.

"What are you doing to earn money?" Nana Abu asks. "I can give you the money."

But as my grandfather reaches into his wallet, Baba stops him. "That's very generous, Abu, but Zara agrees that she needs to learn the value of a dollar. Right, Zara?"

"Right."

"We'll still help you," Naano whispers to me loudly enough that everyone can hear.

"This is spicy!" Zayd complains. He pokes at the curry on his plate and eats only the plain steamed rice next to it.

Naano's attention switches to him right away. It's her life's mission to feed Zayd and fatten him up. But that's because he's so skinny that even strangers comment about it. Like last weekend, we were walking into a restaurant. Zayd's so light, the automatic doors wouldn't open when he stepped in front of them. A man who was standing there laughed so hard that he could barely get out the words, "You need to eat more, little man!"

"Here, let me take the chicken pieces out of the sauce

for you so it's less spicy," Naano says. "You want some gulab jamun, don't you? Eat up like a good boy."

Jamal Mamoo looks at me and winks. And then, to make sure no one brings up my bike again, he changes the subject.

"Ami and Abu, you have a big anniversary coming up soon," he says.

"That's right." Mama clasps her hands together. "Forty years, mashallah! What are we going to do to celebrate?"

"We don't have to do anything big," Naano says. "I just want to go on a cruise. To Alaska. Like my friend Safia did. She put so many pictures on the Facebook, and it's so beautiful."

"That sounds amazing, Ma," Jamal Mamoo says, and chuckles. "But we all can't pick up and go on an Alaskan cruise in a couple of weeks! We can help you plan that for the two of you in the future, inshallah. But we want to do something special with you as a family."

"Oh. Well, then, we can have a nice dinner, like this." Naano looks down at her plate. "Or maybe with some different food."

"You don't like the curry?" Mama frowns.

"No, no, it's very nice, if you add a little salt. And some ghee next time," Naano explains, and quickly pats Mama's hand. "But we could get something from Ravi Kabob so no one has to cook. Or maybe I can cook."

"You're not cooking, Ma," Jamal Mamoo says. "We need to have a proper party. This is a big deal—forty years!"

"Okay," Naano agrees while Nana Abu eyes the gulab jamon on the counter.

"Can you get the small bowls?" Mama asks me.

I pull out the dessert bowls and realize that Naano has the same ones at her house. She has a *lot* of decorations piled up in her cabinet and displayed on the tables in her living room. She's always worried Zayd will break them when he's running around or throwing things. But I bet she doesn't need or want all of them. Maybe she can give me more things for my business. And then I'll be one step closer to riding with my friends, and not having to talk about how I lost my bike again.

"Are we coming over this weekend?" I ask her as I pass out the bowls.

Nana Abu scoops two gulab jamun into his bowl, and Mama jabs her finger toward it. "That's a lot of sugar, Abu," she reminds him gently.

"Yes, of course, come. I'll make you something."
Naano smiles.

I watch as Nana Abu quietly reaches for the big bowl
of gulab jamon again as everyone else starts to eat their
sweet fried dough balls in syrup. He looks so happy that
I don't say a word.

CHAPTER 7

* * *

I rush home from the bus stop the next day and wait for Naomi to get home. She and her older brother, Michael, go to the Jewish Day School instead of my elementary school. Since they don't have a bus, their mom picks them up. The only good thing about Naomi getting back later than me is that I have time to finish a snack before she arrives.

Mama is cutting some apples into slices and scoops some peanut butter onto a plate when I walk into the kitchen.

"How was your day?" she asks, kissing me on top of my head as I wash my hands.

"Good."

"Did you finish your lunch, Zayd?" Mama asks as she unzips his lunch bag.

Zayd nods, but when Mama holds up his sandwich pouch, most of it is still in there.

"I cut off the crust completely like you said," Mama complains. "It's the tiniest sandwich. What am I going to do with you?"

"Maybe we could get other things in our lunches besides sandwiches," I suggest as I crunch on an apple.

"Oh yeah?" Mama turns around and faces me. "Like what?"

I think of all the less-boring foods my friends at school bring for lunch.

"Like noodles, rice, dumplings, samosas."

Mama laughs. "You want samosas?" she says. "I used to beg Naano for turkey sandwiches when I was your age. I didn't want anything Pakistani in my lunch box. Times have changed."

"Yuck. I don't want samosas." Zayd wrinkles his nose

at the apple and reaches for a graham cracker. "They have peas inside."

I walk to the fridge to get some water and notice Michael's bar mitzvah invitation stuck with a magnet. I didn't pay attention to it before, but it's got fancy gold letters and a photo of him wearing a tie on it.

"We should make a nice invitation for the anniversary party for Naano and Nana Abu like this one," I suggest. "And have it in a hall like Michael's thing."

"Isn't his bar mitzvah at the synagogue?" Mama asks.

"Yeah, but they have a party room. Michael said there's going to be a deejay and a magician and lots of decorations."

Michael's been working hard since this summer, going to extra Hebrew lessons to prepare. He told me that the bar mitzvah is when he becomes an adult in the Jewish religion, even though he's only thirteen. I can tell that he likes the idea of being an adult, although right now his voice is all weird. Sometimes it's deeper than usual, and then all of a sudden he'll squeak. Naomi and I try not to laugh, and

I hope it doesn't happen when he has to read Hebrew in front of a room full of people sitting in the temple.

"That's not a bad idea, to have the party in a hall somewhere. We could invite their friends, and cater from a restaurant," Mama says.

"Naano likes Ravi Kabob," I remind her.

"Maybe," Mama says. "I'll talk to Jamal."

My doorbell rings, and it's Naomi, holding a bag of mini-pretzels and a megaphone.

"Ready to sell?" she asks me through the megaphone. I cover my ears to shield them from the blast of sound.

"Ready," I reply. The truth is, I couldn't stop thinking about the business all day. We never figured out how to play music from the wagon, but Naomi's dad said we could borrow his megaphone to get people's attention. It'll definitely do that. Plus we came up with a new name for the business. It's called the Treasure Wagon. Jade and Gloria helped make us a glittery sign to tape onto the side, and it's almost professional.

"Do you want to say it?" I point to the megaphone.

"No, you go ahead." Naomi hands to it me.

"Okay, here we go." I take a deep breath and then speak into the megaphone. "Come on up, everyone. Find amazing treasures, for sale now, at the Treasure Wagon."

We start to walk slowly down the sidewalk, pulling the wagon behind us.

"Don't wait!" I continue. "You don't want to miss out on these one-of-a-kind treasures!"

"Hey, remember what Michael said to say," Naomi reminds me.

"And support kids who are trying to be active," I add, feeling a little weird saying that, even though it's true. It's really just *me* trying to get back onto a new bike.

Melvin comes running out of his house when he sees us. He started kindergarten this year and rides the bus with us in the afternoons.

"What are you doing?" he asks in his chirpy voice. There's a chocolate milk mustache on his upper lip.

"We're selling things for our business, Melvin," Naomi replies.

"No touching," I warn.

"What if I want to buy something?" he asks, looking up at me.

"Do you?"

"Maybe."

"Come on." I nudge Naomi. "Let's keep going."

Melvin points to the antique perfume bottle. It's light green glass with gold designs on it. And there's a golden bulb on top with a thick green tassel hanging off it.

"How much does that cost?"

Naomi picks it up and checks the sticker on the bottom. "It's five dollars."

"*Five* dollars?" Melvin says. "Can I hold it?"

"You seriously want a fancy perfume bottle?" I ask Melvin. He's cute and all, but I want to go around the entire block before it gets dark. And he's delaying us. "What are you going to do with that except break it?"

"It's so pretty," he says, peering at it closer. "It's almost my mom's birthday. Maybe I could get it for her."

"Do you have any money?" Naomi asks.

"No. But I have a loose tooth." Melvin wiggles his bottom tooth, and it moves ever so slightly.

"That's great, Melvin," I say with a sigh.

"So I'm going to get money from the tooth fairy, right?"

"Probably," Naomi says.

I pick up the bottle, wrap it in newspaper, and hand it to him. "Here. Take it."

"Really?" Melvin stops wiggling his tooth.

"Yes. But ask your mom if she wants anything else from our cart. We'll be back around in a bit, okay?"

"I will!" Melvin runs back to his house, trips, and falls. The bottle is still in his hand, and as he jumps up, he checks it.

"It's not broken!" he yells.

Naomi smiles at me. "That was nice of you."

"It's for Mrs. Fu. I know she'll love it."

"Totally," Naomi agrees.

"But now we really need to start selling." I raise the megaphone to my mouth, and we begin walking again.

CHAPTER 8

* ✷ *

My grandparents hate stairs and do everything they can to avoid them. That's why their house is perfect for them. The bedrooms, kitchen, and living room are all on the main level, so they don't have to go downstairs that often. But it also means that whenever we come over, Naano comes up with a big list of things for Zayd and me to do that keeps us running up and down.

"Here you go," Zayd pants. He's carrying a carton of toilet paper half as tall as him.

"There's also laundry in the dryer. Can you bring it up in the blue basket, Zara?" Naano says.

"Okay," I agree, although the laundry room scares me. Zayd and I dare each other to go in there alone and stay inside for two minutes. It's unfinished, with exposed pipes and silver ducts that wind around the exposed wood walls and ceiling. There are weird noises in there, cobwebs, and a musty, dusty smell. Once, Zayd and I were in there looking for old blankets to build a fort with, and I screamed when I suddenly came face-to-face with a dirty ancient doll of Mama's. It had wiry hair and terrifying eyes that blinked if you moved it. And it gave me nightmares for weeks.

"I'm going in now," I announce loudly to nobody as I pull on the string cord that lights up the bulb attached to the ceiling. I make a beeline to the washer and dryer that are around the corner, past the pile of suitcases.

I find the basket, pull open the dryer, and fill it up with the clothes. And then I lift up the basket and turn around to leave.

"WHOA!"

I freeze in my tracks.

There is *so much* stuff in here that I never paid attention to before. It's like I'm seeing all the sagging wooden shelves piled high with boxes and crates for the first time. Plus all the stacks of plastic bins on the ground. There are bags of clothes and toys, and boxes filled with lamps, vases, colorful bowls, and more. I can spot at least two microwaves and a toaster oven.

I'm going to find a million things to sell in here.

As I hoist up the basket and make my way upstairs, I'm already imagining all my new customers. Naomi and I only covered one block in our neighborhood so far, and we had three sales.

Melvin, who took the perfume bottle—even though that was for free.

Mrs. Ratner, who bought the pair of candlesticks for five dollars.

The lady with the husky wanted the globe bookends for six dollars.

That means we've already made eleven dollars. I only have to do that ten or fifteen more times, and I'll have enough money to buy another bike! Maybe I can even get a better one, with a bell and tassels like Jade's. Or one of those extra-special seats.

"Naano!" I say as I come back up the stairs and drop the basket onto the sofa. "You have so much stuff in your storage area. Can I take some of it to sell for my business?"

"Of course." Nana Abu taps my chin as he walks by me. "Take anything you want."

"Downstairs? In the back room?" Mama sighs. "I'm sure there's a lot of junk in there."

"What junk? My things?" Naano sounds worried. "I have to see first."

"Can we look?" I ask.

And then, even though it means a trip down the stairs, Naano huffs and puffs her way down to the basement. She clutches the handrail the whole time.

Mama and I follow her, and when Mama sees the back room, she throws up her hands and lets out an even bigger sigh. And then she starts to lecture Naano.

"Ammi! This has gotten so much messier than the last

time I was down here. Gosh, when was the last time we cleaned up in here? What *is* all this stuff? You don't need all this. When do you ever use it?"

"I do need it." Naano bristles. "You don't worry about my things."

"But what is it? Old appliances? Those don't even work." Mama walks over to one of the boxes and peers inside. "Some of this is really nice stuff, and it's all mixed up with junk."

"It's not junk," Naano grumbles. "These are my things. I told you. You worry about your own house."

"But it's a shame. You should use these things or give them away. Why do you have the old microwave down here? What good does it do?"

Mama is making sense to me, but Naano doesn't want to hear it. She shakes her head and grabs the cracked vase Mama is holding.

"Don't save that," Mama says. "It's broken. Please throw it away."

"You love to throw everything away. Why don't you throw me away too?" Naano complains. She looks so sad all of a sudden that I wish we hadn't brought her in here.

But Mama doesn't back down. She folds her arms in her *I mean business* kind of way. And then she continues to talk to Naano as if she's talking to Zayd or me.

"Ammi, it's not good or healthy to live like this. Think of all the people with so little who could use these things. But it's all sitting here collecting dust." Mama walks over and picks up the creepy doll, which makes me immediately jump back, away from it. "Like this. Why do you still have this thing?"

Naano holds her hand out for it.

"You used to love that doll. You carried it around all day. I caught you and Jamal giving her a bath in the toilet once," Naano remembers.

"You did that?" I laugh, imagining my mom and uncle as little kids.

"Oh, I can tell you stories about your mother." Naano winks at me. "But these are my things. Leave them alone. Come on, let's go upstairs. My legs are hurting and it's time to eat, and Jamal will be here soon."

"What about all of this?" Mama protests.

But Naano ignores her as she rushes out the door, shuffling away from us faster than I've ever seen her move.

CHAPTER 9

✳ ✳ ✳

"Jamal, we need your help," Mama whispers as my uncle comes into my grandparents' house.

"What happened?" Jamal Mamoo whispers back. His big smile is replaced with concern.

"We went downstairs and saw the storage room." Mama's eyes are extra wide and serious.

"And?"

"It's crammed with junk. There's hardly room to move in there. Ammi didn't get rid of any of the things we tried to throw away before."

Jamal Mamoo's smile is back. "That's it? From the look on your face, I thought maybe you found a dead body or something."

"Very funny!" But Mama's lips turn up, even if she doesn't want to laugh right now. "It's really bad."

"Is it?" Jamal Mamoo turns to me.

"It's a lot of stuff," I agree. "I could probably sell some of it and make money. But Naano got really upset when Mama talked about throwing it away or giving it away."

"I can imagine," Jamal Mamoo says. "You need to leave that alone."

"What's all this kuss puss about?" Naano asks as she makes her way over to Mamoo and holds open her arms. "Criticizing your old mother?"

"Of course not." Jamal Mamoo leans over, kisses Naano on the cheek, and squeezes her so tight that she starts to push him away after a moment. "You're the best."

"That's right," Naano grunts. "Don't you forget that. Come, let's eat."

In the kitchen I help Naano scoop the food into

serving dishes. Like usual, she made all our favorites. Biryani, chana, kabobs, and naan. Along with plain rice for Zayd, of course. But today I can't help but notice that some of her dishes are scratched up and stained, and one of them has a chip in it.

"Naano, I saw a platter that was really pretty downstairs," I say. "How come you don't use it?"

"Which platter?" Naano's voice sounds a little suspicious.

"The blue one with the white flowers on it."

"That's for parties."

"When was the last time you had a party, Ammi?" Mama asks as she takes a bowl and carries it to the table.

"I thought it was a party whenever I'm around? I'm offended," Jamal Mamoo teases as he picks a cucumber out of the salad and pops it into his mouth.

"Not with your fingers!" Mama shakes her head at him. "You should use your nice things, Ammi," she adds gently after we sit around the table and start to eat. "What are you saving them for?"

As Mama says that, Naano's face sours like she's tasted something bad. But that's not possible because everything on the table is delicious. And she loves her own cooking more than anyone else's.

"I told you already, leave me alone!" she grumbles.

"What's going on?" Nana Abu looks back and forth at all of us like he doesn't understand.

"Yeah, did I miss something?" Baba turns to Mama with his eyebrows raised.

"Nothing," Mama mumbles.

"You wait until your children come into your house and tell you what to do with your things!" Naano continues, her voice getting louder.

Mama bites her lip. And I quickly wish I'd never said anything about the platter. Although, it is really pretty.

"Let's talk about something else," Nana Abu says. "Zayd, did you do well on your math test?"

"I think so." Zayd nibbles on his naan.

"Have you been practicing your times tables?"

"My what?"

"Abu, they don't teach math the old-fashioned way anymore," Mama says.

"Old-fashioned way?" Nana Abu scoffs. "It's math. There's no fashion to it."

"You should see his math homework. I don't even understand how they teach math now," Baba complains.

And so the conversation turns to multiplication and division and the many ways to get to the same answer. I chime in and try to explain too. All the grown-ups are so confused that Zayd has to get a paper and pencil and show them.

But Nana Abu shakes his head.

"Why are they taking something simple and making it complicated for no reason?" he asks. "We've done basic math the same way for centuries."

"Beats me," Mama says.

"I think it's fun," Zayd says. "I'm good at math. Right, Naano?"

Naano gives him a half smile, sits quietly, and eats

her food. I reach out and squeeze her hand. She squeezes back in a way that I know means she isn't angry with me. But I know she is still upset. And since it's kind of my fault, I hope I can find a way to solve this problem.

CHAPTER 10

*** *** ***

"Mama! We need more stuff!" I yell as I race into the house with Naomi right behind me.

Mama is on the phone and holds up a finger asking us to wait.

"I can't believe we sold so many things!" Naomi says to me, her voice low.

"I know!" I squeeze her arm in excitement. "This is amazing!"

Naomi had the genius idea to add free candy to our cart. Once word got out, through our megaphone, the kids in the neighborhood came running. And then their parents followed. And while they let their kids take lollipops and mini chocolates, they'd notice a frame, paperweight, or tea-pot for themselves. And now, after only a few trips around the block, we're ready for more merchandise.

We stare at Mama, waiting impatiently. Finally she mutes herself.

"What is it, girls? I'm in a meeting."

"We need more things to sell!" I explain. "We're down to the beaded napkin rings and the leaf-shaped bowls that no one likes."

"You took the things from that big box in the garage?"

"Yes."

"And the box labeled 'knickknacks' from the base-ment?"

"Yup. We got them all." There were two boxes in the basement filled with random stuff like cloth napkins, purses, old books, and more.

"Well then." Mama's eyebrows furrow. "I'm sorry I can't help you right now. How about you check in your room?

I'm sure there are plenty of things you can part with."

Naomi turns to me and shrugs.

"Okay," I agree.

"I'll help you," Naomi offers.

I walk into my room, quickly grab the pajamas lying on the floor, and shove them into my hamper.

"How about these?" I pick up my old tap shoes that are too tight for me and show Naomi. The last time I wore them, trying to break a world record, I got the biggest blisters. I wouldn't be sad to see them go.

"Maybe," Naomi says. "But it might be hard to find a customer with the right-sized feet."

"True."

Naomi walks over to my desk and picks up a snow globe with Snoopy and Woodstock hugging inside. "What about this?" she suggests. "Someone might want this."

"Oh no. My uncle got that for me!" I take it from her hand and carefully rest it back on the desk.

"Okay, then how about these?" Naomi walks over and points to a pile of old books on my shelf. "They're kind of

babyish. You probably don't read them anymore."

"Those? Well, not that much." I hesitate. "But I still like looking at the pictures. And my mom and dad used to read those to me when I was little."

"Fine. Do you still want those?" Naomi points to my stuffed animals piled in a corner.

"Well . . ." I shrug. "Kind of."

"All of them?" Naomi asks.

"They're a collection."

"I get it." Naomi flops down onto my bed. "When we moved, my mom made me get rid of so many toys I still wanted. She said we didn't have the space for them."

"What'd you do with them?"

"We donated some. And gave some to my younger cousins." Naomi sighs. "Even though I didn't play with all of them, I still wanted to keep them. I remembered having so much fun with them."

"Did you tell your mom?"

"I tried to. But she said that it was time to let go. And she kept talking about Marie Kondo."

"Who?"

"This lady who's obsessed with cleaning and getting people to fight clutter. She says to only keep things that give you joy. You're supposed to say goodbye to the rest."

"You mean, like, throw them away?"

"No, you're actually supposed to say, 'Goodbye, puzzle. Thank you for giving me something to do on a rainy day' or 'Goodbye, old soccer cleats. Thanks for helping me score that goal,'" Naomi explains.

"Did you actually do that?" I ask. It sounds weird.

"No," Naomi giggles. "I put the things I had to give away into a box and argued with my mom about the rest of it. I cried a lot because we were moving. And I was angry at Marie Kondo."

I bet Naano would have some words for this Marie Kondo. The thought makes me giggle too. But as I study my room, I wonder if Naano feels the same way about her things as I do. Even if she doesn't really need them anymore, maybe they still give her joy. And maybe that's why she isn't ready to let go of them yet.

"Can you say goodbye to this?" Naomi holds up a key chain shaped like a chili pepper from my nightstand that Mr. Chapman, our old neighbor, brought me from Budapest.

"No way. That's full of joy. It's so cute."

"Goodbye to that?" Naomi points to the empty gumball machine on my shelf.

"I love that so much! It used to have joy in it, but I ate all the gumballs."

Naomi moans. "So, what do you want to do, then?"

"Want to get a snack?" I ask her.

"Totally," she agrees.

I grab her arm and link it in mine, happy to leave my room, and everything in it, exactly the way it is.

CHAPTER 11

* * *

I never expected to see a disco ball in a synagogue, but there's one spinning from the ceiling of the party room. A red-faced deejay is set up in the corner, and he's playing a techno version of "Hava Nagila." A bunch of people are dancing in a circle in the middle of the room, holding hands, laughing and singing along. Zayd is dancing his heart out in his suspenders near a little girl in a puffy pink dress.

"Come on!" Naomi notices me standing with Jade and Gloria as she twirls by. The next thing I know, she grabs my hand and the three of us are in the spinning, twisting group with her. I have no idea what I'm doing, but I follow along.

Right then a couple of guys with crew cuts and big muscles bulging out of their dress shirts pick up Michael, who's sitting in a chair, and lift both him and the chair into the air. The circle breaks to let them inside, and then closes around them. Everyone cheers and continues to dance as the young men hold him above their shoulders. Michael is laughing, but his knuckles turn white as he grips the edges of his seat. And although he's grinning, I bet he's as scared as I am that they're going to drop him.

I spot Mama and Baba sitting safely in the corner, talking with Naomi's grandmother. I saw her this morning, during the service in the prayer hall, and she made a big deal about my fancy shalwar kameez. It's the same one I wore on Eid, but Mama insisted that I wear it again today before I outgrow it. And it is really pretty, a seagreen kameez with tiny gold designs on it.

"Oh, that fabric," Naomi's grandma exclaimed when she saw me, like it was the most beautiful thing she'd ever seen. "It's exquisite."

She looks nice herself in a sparkling silver gown that matches her hair, and diamonds. But it felt weird to compliment her right after she complimented me. I didn't want her to think I didn't mean it. So instead I said that it was good to see her again. Which was true. Naomi's grandma lives in a really cool retirement community called Leisure World, but Mrs. Goldstein picks her up every weekend for dinner. We've met a few times before. And she's so nice that I understand why Naomi's family wanted to move to Maryland this summer to be closer to her.

Michael's grandparents, parents, and pretty much all the grown-ups in the room were crying during the bar mitzvah service this morning. Michael stood at the front of the prayer hall, wearing a suit and tie, a white kippah on his head, and a shawl around his shoulders. And I have to admit, he did an impressive job reciting in Hebrew without squeaking once. Michael seemed super nervous and excited at the same time. And his whole family looked so proud.

"This is so beautiful," Mama whispered to me at one point, her voice choked up. "And it's so similar to the mosque, isn't it? We truly are all brothers and sisters." I could see what she meant. Hebrew and Arabic sound a lot alike. The rabbi wore a long beard like our imam. And everyone stood up together at certain times and chimed in to say "Amen" in one voice.

After the service we congratulated Michael as we filed out of the prayer hall and into the reception room. And then instantly everyone who'd been crying moments earlier was hugging, slapping each other on the back, and stuffing their faces with bagels and smoked salmon.

We went home for a few hours to rest and get ready for tonight. And now it's the reception part of the celebration, the one that Michael and Naomi have been talking about for weeks. I already knew a lot of what was going to happen, like the magician that Naomi was completely obsessed with. But the show was amazing. Michael got to assist the magician, who cut open a lemon and found the card Michael had picked rolled up inside!

"Let's get a drink," Naomi says. She wipes the sweat off her forehead, and the girls and I follow her back to the punch bowl.

Michael is there too, recovering from being tossed into the air, and readjusting his kippah. Jade helps him secure it with a bobby pin that she takes out of her own elaborate hairdo.

"This is an amazing party," I tell him. "I still can't get over that magician and the lemon trick."

"I'm going to have to learn how to do that," Naomi says. She's been practicing her own magic routine on the rest of us and holds the neighborhood record for most tricks we can't figure out.

Michael rolls up his sleeves and wipes his face with a napkin. "I'm so glad the hard part went okay this morning and that I can relax and have fun now."

"You were really good," Gloria says. "I can't believe you remembered all those words."

"I was reading them, but thanks." Michael accepts the punch Naomi hands him as the deejay plays the same song for the second time in a row after awkwardly talking into the microphone for a long time. "I think we're cutting the cake soon."

"Are you going to have a bar mitzvah?" Jade asks Naomi.

"Yeah, when I'm thirteen. Except we call it a 'bat mitzvah' for girls," Naomi says, then drains her cup and ladles in more punch. I help myself to more too.

"Do Muslim people have bar and bat mitzvahs?" Gloria asks me.

"No, but when kids finish reading the Quran in Arabic, we have something called an 'Ameen.'"

"Do you read Arabic?" Naomi asks.

"Yeah, but pretty slowly."

"Probably not slower than my Hebrew," Michael says.

"I'm taking notes for my sweet sixteen." Jade waves her hand around. "This is so nice."

"My mom and I are getting lots of ideas for my grand-parents' anniversary party too," I tell everyone.

"Don't hire the same deejay," Naomi whispers. She checks to make sure no one is listening. "He's my cousin. Everyone in the family complains that they have to use him."

"Probably not him." I smile. "But I was thinking that we could play old-timey Pakistani love songs at their party."

"Wait until you hear the speeches during dessert," Naomi says. "My dad's is really goofy."

I make a mental note to ask Mama about speeches. And then while Michael goes to hang out with his friends, all the girls sit down together to eat our slices of the giant mazel tov cake and watch a slide show. There are tons of photos of Michael from different times in his life. We see him as a tiny baby with a younger Mr. and Mrs. Goldstein. Reading a book in his grandmother's lap. Holding baby Naomi. Sitting in the bathtub with lots of bubbles. Holding some kind of trophy. Learning how to ride a bike.

As everyone oohs and aahs over how cute he is, I'm staring at the bike and thinking of when I'll be able to get one. On the drive to the synagogue, I saw one of our reward signs on a lamppost, faded and half-torn. My bike is gone forever, and I hope whoever has it now is taking good care of it. But at least the business has been going great. And now that we're getting closer to having enough money for a new bike, I can't stop thinking about how amazing it's going to feel to ride again.

I also decide that we need a slide show of Naano and Nana Abu for their party.

CHAPTER 12

* ✳ *

"We're going to Radley's," Gloria says when I open the door. "Can you come?"

She's holding her bike helmet, and I point to it. "Remember I don't have—"

"Can you get a ride?" Gloria interrupts.

"I'll ask. When are you leaving?"

"Like, in five minutes?"

"Okay."

Gloria straps on her helmet. "Any idea when you'll get your new bike?" she asks.

"I'm getting closer. We've made eighty-seven dollars. I need at least a hundred and forty."

"But you're splitting the money, right?" Gloria reminds me. "You and Naomi?"

"Right." I sigh. I forgot about that. It's one of the rules. And it's only fair that we share the money, since half the stuff is from the Goldsteins' house, and Naomi does half the work. But that means we need to make double the amount of money.

As Gloria turns to walk down the steps, a lady comes up to the house. She's waving, and as she gets closer to me, I realize she was one of my customers from last week. She lives in the blue house on the street behind ours—the house with colorful flags in the yard decorated with messages about peace and love.

"Excuse me, dear," she says. "I'm glad I caught you."

"Hi," I say, excited to see her. Maybe she wants to buy more things! I remember she picked up one of the beaded napkin rings no one likes.

"I found these, and I think they might be special to your family?" The lady holds out her hand and gives me a stack of photographs.

"You found these?" I repeat as I flip through the photos. They must be from a trip Mama and Baba took a long time ago. Mama's hair is really long, and Baba's is a lot less gray. In one of them Mama is smelling a big pink flower on a bright green bush.

"They were tucked into the middle of the album you sold me, like maybe someone was planning to put them inside at some point," the lady explains.

"Oh."

"Hello, I'm Zara's mother. Can I help you?" Mama comes up behind me.

"Hi, I'm Melissa, your neighbor. I bought an album from Zara a few days ago. And I found those photos inside it and thought you should have them back."

"Album?" Mama grabs the photos from me. "Wait a minute. Oh my goodness! These are from our honeymoon in Costa Rica."

"They're lovely." Melissa smiles. "I hope you don't mind that I looked through them."

Mama tries to smile back, but it's more like she's in

pain. She's frazzled, like when we're late for the dentist and she can't find her keys.

"Zara, where did you get the things you sold?" she asks me, putting her hand on my shoulder and turning me around.

"What do you mean?" I say. "You told me what to take."

"Which boxes did you take them from?" Mama presses.

"The ones in the garage, and the basement. The ones labeled 'knickknacks' and 'keepsakes.' Like you said."

Mama makes a little choking sound. "'Keepsakes' means 'things *to keep*'! That box was filled with special things that you shouldn't have taken!" She clutches at her neck, which turns red as she speaks.

"But 'knickknacks' was okay?" I ask, confused.

"Yes!" Mama moans.

"What does 'knickknack' mean?"

"Like little decorations, or stuff you don't know what to do with. That's why I said you could take them!"

I really wish Mama could have used regular words on her boxes, like "SAVE" and "GIVE AWAY," but I don't say so.

The lady, Melissa, who's been standing there watching us, speaks up again. "It looks like there's been a mix-up. I'll let you figure it out, but I'm happy to return the album, too, if you like?" she says kindly.

"My family friend made that for me," Mama says, sounding like she's in a daze. "I never put photos in it because I was saving it. It would mean a lot to me to have it back. And of course we'll return what you paid for it, with our apologies."

"And you can take whatever else you want from the cart that I'm allowed to sell," I add. "Like . . . those napkin rings? Those aren't a keepsake, are they, Mama?"

"What? Those? Oh, no," Mama says.

"I'm okay, sweetie," Melissa says quickly. "Do you want to come with me and fetch the album?"

"I'm so sorry about this," Mama adds. "Thank you for coming by, and for bringing these back."

"Oh, no worries." Melissa waves her hand. "That's what neighbors arc for. I'm glad it all worked out."

"I'll be right there with your money," I tell Melissa as she walks away.

I slowly raise my eyes to Mama, who seems like she doesn't know whether to laugh or cry. I'm hoping she laughs. But then Mama says, "And then you need to go to everyone else who you sold to, and get everything else back."

"All of it? Even the candy?"

"No, Zara. Just the keepsakes. Not the knickknacks. Or the candy."

"But, Mama, we got lots of—"

"Zara!" Mama's tone makes me stop arguing.

I'm going to wait a little while to ask her which things are keepsakes and which are knickknacks. But my heart sinks as I realize that along with getting the stuff, we're going to have to return at least half the money we made. That stinks! Naomi isn't going to be happy about this either.

Speaking of Naomi, I suddenly remember that my friends, the ones who still have bikes, are waiting for me at the park. But now I don't think it's the right time to ask for a ride.

CHAPTER 13

* ❋ *

I ring the doorbell and take a deep breath. The lady with the purple octagon-shaped glasses opens the door and holds back her barking dog.

I smile brightly at her.

"Hi. Remember me? You bought some pillow covers from me last week?"

"Are you selling more things, because I'm afraid this isn't—" The lady frowns and grabs the dog by the collar as he tries to run outside.

"No, I actually need to get the pillow covers back," I quickly say.

"I'm sorry? What?" The lady steps outside now and closes the door behind her.

Naomi is standing behind me, and she takes a step forward.

"We made a mistake and sold some things that we weren't supposed to," she volunteers.

"A mistake?" The lady scratches her head while the dog howls from behind the screen door.

"They were keepsakes that belonged to my mom. Special things that she didn't want me to take. From her wedding and stuff," I explain.

The lady doesn't say anything as she waits for me to finish.

"Here's your money." I hand her five dollars. "I'm really sorry, but do you mind returning the covers?"

"No," the lady says.

"No?" I say, and turn to Naomi, whose eyes are round with panic.

"No, I don't mind," the lady clarifies. "Wait right here. I'll get them."

Phew!

The lady goes back into her house, and a few minutes later she sticks her hand out the door to pass me the covers. They're cream colored with little orange and green flowers and tiny mirrors sewn into them. Mama told me they were handmade in Pakistan, from the mountainous region, and are worth way more than five dollars. But most important, she got them when she went to visit her relatives in Pakistan, and they were a gift from one of her great-aunts. I inspect them, and other than a few dog hairs, they're as good as new. I mean, as good as old.

"Thank you!" I yell through the door as Naomi checks pillow covers off the list of all the things we had to collect. And I add the pillow covers to the wagon.

"Those were the last things," she says. "We did it."

"I'm really sorry, Naomi," I tell her as a flood of disappointment washes over me. "We did such a great job selling all this stuff, and now this happened."

Naomi shakes her head. "It's okay," she says. "It was an honest mistake."

I swallow hard and nod at my friend, grateful that she's

so understanding. When I told her what had happened, and what I had to do, she was totally ready to help. And when I said that she could keep all the money left from the other things we'd sold, she insisted that we still split it.

"Those are the rules," she said.

"What should we do now?" I ask her.

"Do you want to keep trying with the Treasure

Wagon?" Naomi asks. "I think our customers might be done with us."

"I think so too."

Naomi shrugs. "It was still fun."

"Yeah." I didn't reach my goal, and I still don't have a bike. But it honestly was a good time before today.

"Want to play in the clubhouse?" Naomi asks.

"Sure."

"We can come up with other business ideas," Naomi adds. "We could do things like dog walking, or raking leaves."

"I guess the leaves are going to start falling soon," I sigh. "Should we make a list on the whiteboard?"

"Totally."

I'm sure we'll figure something out soon.

As we get to the house, Melvin sees us and comes running out.

"Do you have any more candy?" he asks.

"Here." Naomi hands him our last lollipop, and when he smiles, I see that his wiggly tooth is gone.

"Did your mom like her birthday present?" I ask.

"She loves it!" Melvin says.

"That's great, Melvin," I say.

Luckily, that wasn't something we had to get back. It was from the knickknack box. But I'm guessing it's already a special keepsake for Mrs. Fu.

CHAPTER 14

* ✳ *

Mama glances at me in the rearview mirror as she drives us to Naano's house.

"I owe Naano an apology," my mother says.

"Why?" I ask from the back seat of the minivan, where I'm sitting next to Zayd and trying to hear over the beeping electronic toy in his hand.

"I wasn't very nice to her the last time we visited. You know, when we talked about all the stuff she's been saving."

"Oh yeah, that," I agree. "You weren't nice at all."

I can tell Mama is smiling even though I can only see her eyes in the mirror, by the way they crinkle in the corners.

"You helped me realize it when you sold my things to the neighbors," Mama continues. "I'm kind of glad that happened."

"You're glad I sold the keepsakes?" I'm finally getting the hang of her strange words, but now I'm confused again. Mama's happy I sold them? She definitely wasn't happy *before* I got everything back.

"A little bit," Mama explains. "The idea of those things being gone forever made me sad. And now I understand how Naano feels about her things."

"All of them?"

"Well, no," Mama says, laughing. "I still don't know why she wants to hold on to an old toaster oven that doesn't work anymore."

"Maybe she thinks she can fix it," Zayd suggests through the beeps.

"Maybe," Mama says. "You know, in Pakistan people

aren't as quick to throw things away as we are here. They fix all sorts of things and make them last for a long time. You find really old things there, like ancient cars and bikes on the road, still being used."

I think about the bike that we threw away, but it was beat-up pretty bad. Could someone have fixed it?

Mama pauses, lost in her thoughts, before she starts speaking again.

"And in Pakistan kids don't have nearly as many toys as you two do. Instead they take care of what they have—"

"Can I have a snack?" Zayd asks, wisely changing the subject.

"Naano will have something for you when we get there," Mama says, and we turn into the neighborhood.

I'm sure Naano will have many things for us. It's one of the best things about going to visit her.

Sure enough, when we arrive, Naano already has a table set with chai for her and Mama and milk for Zayd and me. There are plates of cookies, cut up fruit, and a covered dish.

"Where's Abu?" Mama asks as we hug Naano.

"He's visiting Uncle Shereef. He'll be back soon."

"I'm hungry," Zayd says.

"I made you sweet noodles," Naano says, uncovering the dish to reveal a milky dessert as Mama leads Zayd to the sink to wash hands.

"Yes!" Zayd pumps his fist.

"Remember you still have to have dinner," Mama warns as Zayd helps himself to a huge spoonful of what we call seviyaan and Zayd calls sweet noodles.

"After your snack can you bring in the bags from the trunk?" Mama asks me.

I shove another cookie into my mouth, drink the last of my milk, and head back outside. When the trunk pops open, I see three big HomeGoods bags and exhale in relief. Mama went there without us. Zayd and I *hate* trips to HomeGoods. It's filled with things our parents find fascinating—like frying pans, bedsheets, and pillows—and is basically the most boring place in the world.

I bring in the bags, and Zayd sees them and cringes.

"HomeGoods?" he whispers. "Yuck."

Naano's eyebrow goes up when she sees the bags too. "What's this?" she asks Mama.

"I bought you some baskets, and nice containers," Mama explains. She rummages through the first bag and takes out a brown woven basket that's lined with a flowery fabric.

"Why?" Naano sounds suspicious and holds the basket away from her, as if it's going to bite.

"I felt bad for what I said the other day about your things in the storage room," Mama says. "I'm sorry. You should keep whatever makes you happy."

"Humph," Naano grunts, which I think means she accepts Mama's apology.

"You know, Mama, you sound like Marie Kondo," I say.

"Marie Kondo?" Mama laughs. "What do you know about her?"

"I know she says to only keep the things that bring you joy."

"That's right." Mama smiles. "And I thought we could help you sort through your things, Ammi, and put them in some new containers, for extra joy."

"Humph," Naano repeats, but I can tell she's pleased. And when we head into the storage room, she lets me fill a paper grocery bag with some empty boxes to recycle. Plus she makes a tiny pile of things she is considering getting rid of.

"Naano, do you want to have a garage sale?" I offer. "We can help you."

"What happened to your wagon business?" Naano asks.

"We're not doing that anymore." I sigh.

Naano gives me a sideways glance and says "We'll see" at the moment Mama squeals.

"I can't believe this!" Mama holds up a bright orange shoebox.

"Nikes?" Zayd asks.

"No, it's a diorama I made. Oh my goodness! I must have been in third grade. There's so much detail. This is supposed to be our mosque. I was trying to show my family celebrating Eid."

Mama's eyes grow glassy as she touches each of the things that she made so long ago. "There's the imam, and there's me, wearing a shalwar kameez. And Jamal in his little topi. Wow, I must have been around your age when I made this," she says to us.

"It's cute, Mama," I say while Naano grunts in a way that I know means, *Look who's enjoying the old stuff now.*

We keep stopping whenever someone finds another item that brings up another story, so we don't get too far with the sorting. But Naano sits in an old folding chair and doesn't complain or say she wants to stop. And Zayd and I learn a lot about our family.

As I'm sorting through one of the boxes in the corner, I find a couple of thick envelopes. Inside are stacks of photographs, and a sleeve of tiny black strips with holes in the sides. They're more old photos, of Mama and Jamal Mamoo when they are kids, and Naano wearing her hair in a big bun. She's glamorous.

"Find something good?" Naano asks as she shuffles toward me.

"Mostly old papers," I say, and I quickly slip the envelopes into a bag so she doesn't see. I don't think Naano will miss them if I borrow them for a few days.

CHAPTER 15

I ring Jade and Gloria's doorbell and wait. Mrs. Thomas answers the door with a smile.

"Hi, hon. Hard at work selling again?"

"Not anymore," I say. "Can Jade and Gloria play?"

Jade pokes her head out the door a second later. "Hey, Zara."

"Hey, Jade. I need your help with a craft project."

"Craft?" Jade perks up. "What kind?"

I fill her in, and she listens thoughtfully.

"Meet me in the clubhouse in five minutes. I'll get some supplies."

When we are all assembled in the clubhouse, I show the girls the album, the special keepsake one that Mama was saving, and the photos that I took from Naano's house.

"Did your mom say we can use the album?" Naomi asks.

"Yes, I made sure this time," I explain. "And don't worry, I asked if I could use the photos, too."

"Okay good," Naomi says.

"I want to make my grandparents a special gift for their anniversary party. I saw how everyone loved the old photos of Michael at his bar mitzvah, and my uncle is going to put together a slide show like that too. But I wanted to give them something for them to keep, after the party is over."

"Okay, so what can we do?" Gloria asks.

"Well, I want to make it extra nice, with memories, decorations, and other things mixed into the pages. I know you all are good at that kind of thing."

"Totally!" Jade is already concentrating hard as she flips through the album. "Maybe we could add pages with stories and put in some captions?" she says.

"Yes!" I clap.

"And maybe some stickers? Or clip art?" Gloria adds.

"We have leftover cards from the bar mitzvah," Naomi offers. "We can cut them up and make gold letters."

"Perfect." I smile. "I'll collect the stories from my mom and dad and uncle. I already know one about that doll." I point to a photo of Mama as a little girl, holding the scary doll. Naano was right that she carried it around with her wherever she went. It's in many of the photos.

"Is that you?" Gloria asks. She holds up a photo of Naano holding a newborn baby in a blanket.

"Maybe? Me or Zayd. Is there a date on it?" I ask.

"No."

"I'll ask my mom if she knows," I say.

BANG! BANG!

"Who is it?" Gloria checks the door. "Oh, it's Zayd. What is it, Zayd?"

"Can I come in?"

"There's no room . . . Ooh . . . okay . . . ," Gloria says as Zayd squeezes past her and comes inside.

"Zayd, can you please not bother us? We're busy," I say.

"What are you doing?" He starts to touch the stickers and markers that Jade brought.

"Nothing. Can you go play with Melvin? Or Alan?" I try to gently nudge him toward the door, but for someone so skinny he's like a statue that won't budge.

"What's that picture of Naano for?" Zayd peeks at everything spread out on the folding table.

I sigh. "It's a surprise for Naano and Nana Abu. You can't tell them, okay?"

Zayd zips up his lips with his fingers. "Can I do some cutting? I'm good at cutting!" he asks.

"Sure, Zayd," Naomi says. "But do you have safety scissors?"

"Yeah."

"Can you get them? And some other very important supplies?" She looks over at me and winks.

"Like what?" Zayd asks.

"Some glue sticks, three paper clips, and a cup of warm water," Naomi says.

"And can you get us some snacks?" Gloria adds.

"All that? I can't carry so much," Zayd complains.

We keep him busy running back and forth bringing

us what we need as we trim, glue, fold, and color the pages we're adding into the album. Jade shows us how to make little frames for each of the photographs, so they really pop. And then we use her fancy label maker to print out captions.

In the end the album is bursting with color, memories, and joy.

Naano is going to love it.

CHAPTER 16

"Please, everyone, can you take your seats?" Jamal Mamoo clinks a spoon against the side of his water glass to get all the guests' attention.

The buzz of the room slowly turns into a few whispers as my uncle clears his throat and continues. "We are so honored to have you all with us tonight as we celebrate a wonderful occasion, the union of my dear parents for the past forty years, mashallah."

I hear echoes of "Mashallah" in the crowd.

"We want to thank you for being a part of this special

night and celebrating the happy couple. But you've heard enough of my voice, so how about you join me in demanding that we hear from the lovebirds themselves." And then Jamal Mamoo starts to chant "SPEECH! SPEECH! SPEECH!" along with a bunch of the gray-haired aunties and uncles in the crowd.

Naano's face turns red, and she shakes her head as Mamoo gestures toward her and Nana Abu. But after Baba encourages him, my grandfather finally gets up, shuffles to the stage, and takes the microphone.

"Thank you all for being here," he begins, looking as handsome as ever in his black suit and red tie. "I want to tell you all that it's one hundred percent true what they say about marriage. . . . Happy wife, happy life."

He smiles after a long pause. "But what they didn't say is that my life wouldn't be happy without the greatest wife in the world. And I thank Allah every day for my wife, my children, my beautiful grandchildren, and our dear friends. I'm so glad we are all together and could enjoy each other's company and this delicious food."

He pauses again and looks at Naano. "Of course, it wasn't quite as delicious as the food my greatest wife makes me every day. But it was tasty. And now, did I hear someone say that it's time for dessert?"

Everyone claps and laughs and cheers, and Nana Abu bows his head and puts his hand on his heart before shuffling back to the table. Zayd gives him a big high five, and I hear him through the applause say, "Good job, Nana Abu!"

Naano's face is red again as Nana Abu pats her hand when he sits down next to her. She is radiant in a sparkling cream-and-gold shalwar kameez, and a silky cream dupatta on her hair. Mama and I helped her get ready, and I picked out the jewelry for her to wear. She laughed and said her friends would think she was trying to act like a young lady. But we insisted she wear the earrings and necklace, and I think she's perfect.

The hall is gorgeous too, with the cream and gold balloons Mama and Jamal Mamoo decorated tied to the chairs, and candles and flowers at the center of all of the tables.

"Zara, it's time," Mama says as she comes up to me. "Are you ready?"

"Yes!" I say, heading to the stage area, where I take the microphone and raise it to my lips. "Asalaamualaikum, everyone," I say as I watch Naano and Nana Abu. "We have a little surprise for my grandparents that we put together. I hope you will enjoy these special memories from the past forty years."

Baba made a playlist of old love songs to accompany the slide show we all worked on together. The photos start rolling now on the big screen he set up.

"Baharo phool barsao . . . ," the song plays, and I see Naano's hand go over her mouth. Mama and Baba said this is one of the most romantic songs ever sung, by the legendary Muhammed Rafi. I don't understand the words in Urdu. But when the singer says "mera mehboob aya hai," all the aunties in the room seem to be melting, so I think my parents were right.

I alternate between watching my grandparents' reaction and looking at the grainy photos from their wedding in

Pakistan. Next we see photos of Naano in America, posing in front of a painting, the cherry blossom trees in DC, and a green car parked in the driveway of their house. After a while we see photos of little Mama and then Jamal Mamoo. We made sure to include Mama with the creepy doll, and Jamal Mamoo in his pirate costume. There's a family trip to Pakistan; Eid celebrations; dinner parties; and a visit to Mecca, where Nana Abu shaved his head. And then finally, there are photos of Zayd and me. We ended the slide show with as many family photos as we could find.

Naano hardly ever cries, but her eyes are glistening as she watches the screen and clutches Nana Abu's arm. At the end she catches my eye and smiles at me, and I know that this night is as special to her as it feels to me.

After the slide show Mama passes out slices of the cake that Naano and Nana Abu cut earlier. Everyone eats the cake, along with chai and gulab jamun that honestly aren't as good as Naano's but are still decent. I help myself to six of them and see that Nana Abu has about as many in front of him.

"You did good," Jamal Mamoo says to me, sliding into the seat next to me. "I think that turned out well, don't you?"

"It was good," I agree. I don't mention that the party would have been slightly more fun with a deejay and a disco ball. Most of the people here are as old as my grandparents, and maybe that would have been too much for them.

When most of the guests have left, Naano and Nana Abu sit on a sofa near the entrance to the hall. They look tired but happy, waiting for Baba to pull up the car.

"We have another surprise for you," I share, while Zayd runs behind the table where we stored our things and pulls out a gift bag. He hands it to Nana Abu, who pulls out the tissue paper that's on top, one piece at a time. And then he starts to fold it into neat squares.

After the third piece, Zayd impatiently throws out the rest and helps Nana Abu slide the album out of the bag.

"What's this?" Naano asks.

"It's all the photos from the slide show," I explain. "With stories and captions mixed in."

Naano and Nana Abu fall silent while they slowly flip through the pages. Every now and then they point to show the other something, and I hear Nana Abu chuckle and Naano murmur in Urdu. Naano turns each page gently, like it's made of glass. When they're done with the last page, she closes the album and clutches it to her chest.

"Thank you," she says, motioning for Zayd and me to come closer. "This is the best gift I could ever have. Other than . . . the two of you."

She kisses us both before adding, "Now let's take a selfie."

CHAPTER 17

* ✳ *

"That's the last of it," Baba says as he brings me another box of stuff from the basement.

"I don't have any more room!" I moan. "Look!"

The three folding tables we've set up outside are already overflowing with things to sell at Naano's garage sale. I tried to divide them up into decorations, useful things, and things I don't think anyone will want. We put stickers on everything with the prices we came up with earlier. And I made a list of rules for everyone working the sale, with Mama's help.

- Greet everyone who comes and offer them a snack.

- If someone likes something but doesn't seem sure, tell them why it's so great.

- Offer to plug in any electronics in the garage to show that they work.

- Don't lower any prices without checking with Naano first.

We advertised on the neighborhood discussion board and hung signs up around the block. And even though it's only ten a.m., so far we've had a bunch of Naano's neighbors stop by and at least seven cars come through. I've sold a ceramic owl, hand towels with pears embroidered on them, a set of encyclopedias from 1978, a bunch of magnets, and a lampshade.

"How much for this?" a man with a leather jacket asks, pointing to the toaster oven sitting on the table of things I don't think anyone will want.

"Um, I think that's ten dollars," I reply. "But I have to warn you, it turns on, but you have to unplug it to turn it off."

I heard the story about how Jamal Ma
bought Naano a replacement toaster ov
after hearing her complain about all the
bread Nana Abu was burning. But since
this one still technically worked, Naano
saved it in the basement. It was her
backup toaster.

The man opens it up, peers inside, and
moves the tray in and out.

"I'll take it," he says.

"Are you sure?" I ask, which makes
Jamal Mamoo smirk from where he's
stacking old comics that belonged to him.

"Yes. And that set of salad tongs."

"Okay, great," I say as he hands me tv
dollars.

As the man walks back to his car with his purchases,
Jamal Mamoo erupts into his loud wacky laugh. "You're
not supposed to talk customers *out of* buying things,
Zara!" he says.

"I know, I know," I laugh. "You already told me. One man's trash is another man's treasure."

We take a lemonade break and count the money we've made so far: forty-six dollars. Not bad for two hours in the morning.

"There are matching napkins to go with that tablecloth, if you want to see," I hear Naano say to a young
woman with a flower tattoo.

"Oh yes, please. These are so pretty," the woman says.

"They are handmade," Naano adds.

"Oh really? From where?" The woman smiles.

"Pakistan," Naano says. She pronounces it the way
Pakistanis say it: *pock-iss-tohn*. The woman nods even
though I get the feeling she doesn't know where in the
world Naano is talking about.

"I'll take them all," she says.

"Do you want to see some pillow covers? Also handmade?" Naano asks.

It's like Naano was born to be a salesperson. By the
time she's done, the flower tattoo woman takes the tablecloth, napkins, pillow covers, two wooden carved boxes,
and six serving spoons.

Meanwhile Zayd keeps finding things he wants us to
take home. He's missing the whole point of this garage
sale.

"How about this?" He holds up a hair dryer that's shaped like a helmet. "It's so cool."

"No, Zayd," Mama says. "We don't need that."

"Then can I have this?" He points to a small denim-colored case with a handle.

"No," Mama says. "What do you need a record player for?"

"Record player? Wait a minute. Does it still work? I want that!" Jamal Mamoo opens it up and peeks inside. "Sweet! Let's see if it works." He carries it over to the garage and tries to plug it into the outlet in the wall.

"There's no needle," Nana Abu warns. "It won't play your records."

"I can get a needle." Jamal Mamoo rubs his hands together. "And then I can listen to vinyl."

"For you, it's fifty dollars," Naano declares, and all of us laugh.

By the end of the day, we've managed to clear out a good amount of stuff. And Jamal Mamoo isn't the only one with something to take home. Mama wants a quilted dome that goes on top of a teapot, Baba found a wire cutter and a set of metal hooks, and Zayd has a flattened leather soccer ball that's brand-new and only needs to be pumped up.

"What about you, Zara?" Mama asks. "You don't want anything?"

"Yeah, Zara, what about this?" Jamal Mamoo picks up Mama's creepy old doll and pretends to make it speak in a high-pitched voice. *"Why don't you love me?"*

"Not that! It's so scary." I giggle. But that only encourages my uncle to act like the doll is coming to life and trying to grab me with its tiny arms. I scream and run around the yard as he chases me.

"I think Zara might want this," Naano says, holding out a wad of money as I race over to hide behind her. "The garage sale was your idea, so you deserve it."

"No, no, Ammi." Mama starts to shake her head. "Everyone helped out, and it was your things that sold. You should keep the money."

"Choop!" Naano scolds. "Thanks to Zara, I'm going

to use so many things that have just been sitting downstairs. And it feels good to clean out that room after so long. Take it." She waves the money in my direction.

"Thanks, Naano. Are you sure?" I ask as I take it. Then I turn to Mama and shrug in a *What can I do if my grandmother wants to give me cash?* kind of way.

"I'm sure, beti. You made me realize that the best thing to save is memories. I don't need all of this junk."

Mama looks at me when Naano says "junk" and grins.

"What do you want to do with everything that didn't sell? Take it back down?" Baba asks.

"No, no," Naano says. "Take the nice things to the donation center. And throw away what you think no one will want."

The words are barely out of her mouth before Mama and Jamal Mamoo start to load up the minivan, quick, before she changes her mind.

CHAPTER 18

✳ ✳ ✳

"Isn't this place the coolest?" I ask Naomi.

"There's so much stuff here," she says, scanning the room, which is crammed with goods from the floor to the ceiling. This donation center is like Naano's storage room, but bigger and more organized.

When I came with my mom and Jamal Mamoo the first time, I thought the nice lady in a gray hijab would send us away. It didn't seem like there was any more room for Naano's additions. But she told us to leave the boxes and bags in the corner, said "Jazakallah khairun," and handed us a receipt.

"Everything here is donated," I explain to my friend. "And if you buy stuff, the money goes to mosque programs that help families in the community."

"That's great," Naomi says. "Should we give her our things?"

Naomi and I decided to donate the leftover items from the Treasure Wagon that we never sold. Mama added extra things from home after sorting through cabinets and the garage. And I decided I could part with some of my toys and books that I don't use, that someone else could be reading and playing with.

When we were leaving the house, Mama said that Naomi could come with us, and that we could get some ice cream afterward. And so here we are.

"Asalaamualaikum," the lady says, and smiles at me. Her hijab is blue today. "Back again?"

"Waalaikumussalaam," I say, and smile back. "We have some more things to donate."

"Wonderful, thank you." The lady motions for us to leave the items and hands Mama a receipt.

"Aww." Naomi picks up a fluffy yellow tutu as we turn

to leave. "I had one like this when I was in second grade."

"Me too," I say. "But mine was purple."

"And ooh, check that out." Naomi runs over to a table and points to a bell. It's the kind that goes on a bike. "You could get this for your new bike," she says, ringing the bell.

"Are you interested in a bicycle?" the lady asks me from behind the counter. "There's no room in here, but I have some out back if you want to see?"

I glance at Mama, who raises an eyebrow. "Why not?" she says.

We follow the lady, who opens a back door to a corridor where there's an assortment of bikes, trikes, and scooters leaning against the wall.

"Naomi, look!" I point. There's one bike a little bit apart from the others. It's kind of like the one I lost—the right size and shape, but dark red instead of turquoise.

"What do you think?" I ask her.

"It's nice." Naomi goes close to it and inspects it more closely. "A few scratches, but not too bad."

"Yeah." I kick at the wheels, check the chain, and

study the bike for a moment. This might actually . . . work.

"Can I sit on it?" I ask the lady.

"Sure. You can ride it too, if you like," the lady offers.

I throw my leg over the bike and straddle it. The handlebars are solid and even have white tassels hanging off them, like Jade's bike.

"This could be the one!" Naomi says, and claps her hands.

"Let's see how it rides first," I say with a laugh. But as I sit on the seat and start to pedal, I instantly feel the same thrill I felt on my fancy new bike. This one is as quiet and smooth, and best of all, it can let me ride with my friends and go to Radley's again.

I ride to the end of the corridor and back. And then I stop.

"How much is it?" I ask the lady.

"I think I could give it to you for fifty dollars," she says. "Especially since you've brought in so many things."

"Are you sure, Zara? It's not the new bike you've been

wanting," Mama warns. "I want you to be happy with whatever you get."

"Do you think I can get a new clip for a water bottle?" I ask.

Mama smiles. "I think so."

"And a new water bottle with my name on it?"

"Of course."

"Don't forget a new lock," Naomi adds.

"Right." I giggle.

"Would you like it, then?" the lady asks. "I can throw in the bell for you."

"Yes, please."

I pull out the wad of cash that Naano gave me and count fifty dollars. Mama puts her hand on my shoulder and squeezes, and I know she approves. Maybe this isn't the bike I thought I wanted all this time, but I have a feeling it's going to be even better. Because there's already a cool story of where it came from. And I know there will be so many more memories of where it takes me.

And, in the end, that's what really matters.

Acknowledgments

When I was growing up, there was an unspoken rule in my family that we saved anything that might be useful in the future. An empty glass peanut jar could store spices or daal. Shoeboxes had endless potential. The toaster that didn't turn off? I still haven't figured that one out, but into the storage room it went.

That's why I loved exploring the idea of trash versus treasure in this book and the rules about what we keep, reuse, recycle, and more. Like Zara, it's taken me a while to sort it out, but I know now that the things I treasure most aren't *things* at all.

A few of the people who I hold dear, and am grateful to for their help with this book and so much more, include:

My trusted agent, Matthew Elblonk, for believing in my books and entertaining my wild ideas.

My thoughtful editor, Kendra Levin, for her strong storytelling instincts and for pushing me to trust myself.

My incredible illustrator, Wastana Haikal, for depicting Zara in a way I couldn't have imagined, and the team at Simon & Schuster, who work hard to make our beautiful books and get them into the world.

My invaluable writing group, Laura Gehl, Joan Waites, and Ann McCallum, for their collective wisdom.

My patient friends who support me by reading, listening, and advising.

My kind neighbors and friends Nomi and Michael for their company and imaginative games, and their parents, Marion and Tony Pitch, who always made me feel like another member of the family.

My brilliant parents and siblings, who form the basis of many characters in this series, thanks to their humor and colorful personalities.

My wonderful husband and sons for building the memories I hold dearest with me.

My prized readers for picking up my books and making them part of your life.

You are a treasure.